The Berenstain Bears
PLAY T-BALL

Stan & Jan Berenstain

Sandy Creek

Sandy Creek
122 Fifth Avenue
New York, NY 10011

ISBN 978-1-4351-2654-1
Manufactured in China.
Manufactured 05/2010
Lot 10 11 12 13 SCP 10 9 8 7 6 5 4 3 2

Brother and Sister Bear

were helping some smaller cubs.

They were helping them

learn to play T-ball.

There were two teams:

the Bluebirds and the Cardinals.

Brother and Sister

coached both teams.

Mr. Gump was the ump.

"Batter up!" said Mr. Gump.

"Up where?" said Billy.

"Up to the plate—

I mean up to the tee," said Brother.

"I don't see any plate.

I don't see any 'T,'" said Billy.

"*This* tee," said Sister.

"Watch me hit the ball."

WHACK! It went far.

It was Billy's turn.

He put the ball on the tee.

He swung the bat.

He swung hard.

But he hit the tee
instead of the ball.

BOI-N-N-NG went the tee.

Dribble, dribble went the ball.

"Run to the base!" said Brother.

Billy ran to the base.

"First base, not second base!"

said Sister.

10

Billy started to run

back to first base.

A Bluebird player

tagged him with the ball.

"You are out!" said the ump.

"Out?" asked Billy.

"What do you mean?

We are all out."

"We are all *outside*,"

said Brother.

"But that is not what *out*

means in T-ball."

"You mean I'm out of the game?"

asked Billy.

He began to cry.

"Please don't cry," said Sister.

She took him to the bench.

"You just sit here for a while."

"Batter up!" said the ump.

It was Jill's turn to bat.

Jill hit the ball hard.

It went far.

"Good hit, Jill!" said Brother.

"Now run," said Sister.

"First, you run to first base."

Sister ran to first base with her.

She ran to second base with her.

She ran to third base with her.

"Good!" said Sister.

"Now, run home."

Jill ran home.

She lived at 414 Walnut Street.

"No!" said Sister.

Brother ran after Jill.

He brought her back.

"Not *that* home," said Brother,

"*this* home!"

Before Jill could touch home,

a Bluebird got the ball.

"Tag her!" said Brother.

The Bluebird tagged her.

"You are *it*!" he said.

Then he ran away.

Jill ran after him.

"No!" shouted Brother.

"We are not playing tag!

We are playing T-ball!"

He jumped up and down.

He threw his hat
on the ground.

He jumped on his hat.

The cubs were all running around.

They were playing tag.

Brother and Sister got upset.

"Getting upset will not help,"

said the ump.

"What should we do?" asked Brother.

"A coach is like a teacher,"

said Mr. Gump.

"Teach them how to play."

That is what they did.

Then they had a game.

The Bluebirds won.

The score was Bluebirds 27,

Cardinals 26.

Coach Brother and Coach Sister learned a good lesson.

They learned that jumping on your hat never taught anybody anything.